The Audition

"Thanks, girls. We'll just go out to the backyard and discuss the tryouts in private before we announce our final decision," Bruce explained. "Come on, guys."

"Don't feel bad if you don't get it, Jess," Elizabeth whispered to her twin. "You tried hard. And I thought you sounded good."

That wasn't exactly true, but Elizabeth thought she might as well say something nice.

"Thanks. I did, too," Jessica said matter-of-factly. "I can't wait for them to announce their decision."

Just then, Bruce and Aaron and the other two boys came back down the steps.

"Wow. That was fast," Elizabeth murmured in surprise.

"We've made our choice," Bruce announced.

"I just know I've got it," Jessica whispered. Elizabeth braced herself for the worst.

SWEET VALLEY TWINS

Jessica, the Rock Star

Written by
Jamie Suzanne

Created by
FRANCINE PASCAL

A BANTAM SKYLARK BOOK®
NEW YORK · TORONTO · LONDON · SYDNEY · AUCKLAND

g
Suz

RL 4, 008-012

JESSICA, THE ROCK STAR
A Bantam Skylark Book / November 1989

*Sweet Valley High® and Sweet Valley Twins are trademarks of
Francine Pascal.*

Conceived by Francine Pascal

*Produced by Daniel Weiss Associates, Inc.,
27 West 20th Street,
New York, NY 10011*

Cover art by James Mathewuse.

*Skylark Books is a registered trademark of Bantam Books, a division of
Bantam Doubleday Dell Publishing Group, Inc.*

ISBN 0-553-15766-3

Published simultaneously in the United States and Canada

*Bantam Books are published by Bantam Books, a division of Bantam
Doubleday Dell Publishing Group, Inc. Its trademark, consisting of
the words "Bantam Books" and the portrayal of a rooster, is Registered
in U.S. Patent and Trademark Office and in other countries. Marca
Registrada. Bantam Books, 666 Fifth Avenue, New York, New York 10103.*

PRINTED IN THE UNITED STATES OF AMERICA

O   0 9 8 7 6 5 4 3 2 1

Jessica,
the Rock Star

One

◆

"Elizabeth, are you awake?"

Elizabeth Wakefield lifted her head from her pillow and peered sleepily into the darkness. "I am now. Is something wrong, Jess?"

"No." Jessica Wakefield hurried through the bathroom that connected her bedroom with her twin sister's and jumped onto Elizabeth's bed. "I'm just too excited to sleep. The concert was so incredible!"

Elizabeth blinked at the light that spilled from the bathroom. She pushed her tangled blond hair out of her face and sat up. The rock concert at Secca Lake, a short drive from Sweet Valley, had been exciting, but exhausting, too. Wouldn't Jessica ever tire of reliving the evening?

"You've told me that ten times already. Don't you know how late it is?"

"Who cares?" Jessica grinned. "Melody

Power is absolutely the greatest rock singer in the whole world!"

"She's good, all right," Elizabeth agreed.

"I love everything about her. And did you notice that she looked right at me when she walked into the spotlight?"

"That's because you were screaming so loud," Elizabeth said with a laugh.

"I still can't believe what great seats we had." Jessica sighed. "I think Melody Power is just too much!"

Elizabeth couldn't help giggling at her sister's enthusiasm. Staring at Jessica's excited face was almost like looking into a mirror. Both twins had long, silky blond hair, sparkling blue-green eyes, and dimples in their left cheeks. But even though they looked identical, their personalities were very different.

Elizabeth was the more serious twin. She loved school, especially English, and hoped to be a writer someday. She had helped found the sixth-grade newspaper, *The Sweet Valley Sixers*, and spent a lot of her free time writing articles for it.

Jessica's favorite activity was talking about clothes and boys. She spent endless hours with her friends from the Unicorn Club, an exclusive group of the most popular girls at Sweet Valley Middle School, gossiping. Jessica was much too busy having fun and engaging in social activities to be concerned with something as trivial as her schoolwork.

But in spite of their differences, the twins were best friends. They always had the most fun when they were together, and tonight was no exception. They had both enjoyed the concert immensely.

"Yes, she really put on a good show tonight," Elizabeth whispered. "But you'd better not talk so loud. Mom and Dad let us stay up late to go to the concert, but if they hear that we're still awake—"

"Don't you think I was the greatest to answer that radio quiz correctly?" Jessica interrupted, lowering her voice slightly. "Just think, if I hadn't won those concert tickets, we'd never have been in the front row. We wouldn't even have gotten to go," Jessica reminded her sister.

"I know, Jess. The tickets sold out so fast, we wouldn't have had a chance. Hey, you're not sleeping in your new Melody Power T-shirt, are you?" Elizabeth suddenly asked her twin.

"Sure. Why shouldn't I?"

Elizabeth yawned. "It's just that if you sleep in it, it'll be wrinkled tomorrow. And I know you want to wear it to school."

"Oh, I guess you're right." Jessica jumped up. "I'd better put on a nightgown."

"OK. And get some sleep, too, so you're not too tired to tell Lila and all the other Unicorns every detail of the concert."

"Since you're so anxious to get back to sleep, I guess you're not interested in hearing my great idea."

Elizabeth had already shut her eyes. She opened one cautiously. "What idea?"

"Oh, just that I'm going to be a rock star someday, just like Melody Power!" Jessica skipped happily back to her own room.

Elizabeth ducked under the covers and let out a groan.

"Jessica! Elizabeth!" Mrs. Wakefield called from the bottom of the stairs. "Time to get up."

Elizabeth yawned. How could it be morning already? It seemed like she had gone to sleep only minutes before. It took something really special for the twins to be allowed to stay up late on a school night. They were lucky their parents had agreed that Jessica's free tickets couldn't be wasted. Mr. and Mrs. Wakefield had even listened to the concert on the radio at home last night *and* enjoyed it.

Elizabeth crawled out of bed and opened her

closet door. She pulled out a pair of jeans and a cotton sweater. As she slipped the sweater over her head she wondered if Jessica had gotten any sleep at all.

Elizabeth grinned, remembering how Jessica had warbled her imitation of Melody's new hit all the way home from the concert. She was just bubbling over with excitement. Elizabeth was sure it would take her twin a few days to come back down to earth.

Is Jessica out of bed yet? she wondered. The sound of running water in their connecting bathroom answered her question. Elizabeth would comb her hair and brush her teeth later. Right now, the smell of breakfast was making her stomach growl. She hurried toward the stairs.

When she entered the sunny, Spanish-tiled kitchen, she saw her mother standing in front of the stove, making scrambled eggs. Her older brother, Steven, had already wolfed down his meal. He had a couple of textbooks tucked under one arm and was heading for the door.

"Did you have enough to eat?" Mrs. Wakefield asked him.

Steven's hearty appetite was a family joke. He swallowed a bite from the piece of toast in his free hand and nodded. "Got to run. I told the guys I'd come early to shoot some baskets." He grabbed two more pieces of toast and hurried out the door.

Mrs. Wakefield put some eggs and a piece of toast on a plate and placed it in front of Elizabeth.

"I'm glad you were able to pull yourself out of bed," she said. "I was worried about you and Jessica staying up so late."

Elizabeth picked up her fork and tried to look alert. "I'm really glad you let us go to the concert, Mom. It's not every day we get the chance to see a real live rock star. Especially with front-row seats!"

Mrs. Wakefield smiled. "I know. Your father and I agreed that forbidding you to go to the concert would be unfair. Besides, it would have broken Jessica's heart."

"You can say that again. She was so excited she could hardly sleep last night." Elizabeth took a forkful of her eggs. She realized it might not be wise to tell her mother just how late Jessica had been up reliving the concert.

Mrs. Wakefield glanced toward the hallway. "Is Jessica out of bed?"

"She was in the bathroom," Elizabeth said. "She should be down any minute."

Then they both heard the sounds of Jessica's voice coming closer as she hummed Melody Power's latest song. Elizabeth giggled, reaching for the butter.

But when Jessica appeared in the doorway, pausing to make a dramatic entrance, Elizabeth's eyes widened and she forgot all about her breakfast.

Jessica entered the kitchen wearing her new Melody Power T-shirt, her shortest miniskirt, electric-pink tights, and pink high-top sneakers. In addition, it looked as if she had put on every scarf and necklace she owned. It was all too much to believe!

When Elizabeth looked closer, she recognized a few of her own possessions! "Where did you find all that stuff, Jess?" she asked. "That's *my* coral necklace!"

"I knew you wouldn't mind if I borrowed it, Lizzie. Anyway, is that all you can say about my new look?" Jessica asked, sounding hurt. "Don't you think it's great?"

Mrs. Wakefield brought Jessica's plate to the table. "I think you overdid the makeup, Jessica."

"I did not!" Jessica frowned. "It's just like Melody Power's and she's beautiful!"

"Performers need heavier makeup on stage," Mrs. Wakefield explained. "In normal light, that kind of makeup doesn't look quite as effective."

Elizabeth tried not to laugh at Jessica's heavy

layer of lavender eye shadow. "You look like you've got a black eye, Jess."

Mrs. Wakefield handed Jessica a napkin.

Jessica wiped away some of the excess shadow. "When I'm a big star, you'll be sorry you didn't appreciate me." She began to eat.

"Look out. One of your scarves is dipping into your eggs," Elizabeth warned with a giggle.

Jessica sat up a little straighter.

"Better hurry if you want to walk to school with me," Elizabeth said. "I have a newspaper meeting this morning."

Jessica looked up and swallowed a mouthful of egg. "You're not going to write an article for the paper about the concert, are you?" She sounded alarmed.

"Of course."

"But *I* wanted to be the one to tell everybody all about it," Jessica wailed.

"Don't worry," Elizabeth said. "The next edition won't be out until Friday. By that time, everyone in school will have heard your story."

Jessica relaxed. "You're right," she agreed. "Thank goodness!"

Two

◇

Jessica hurried toward the fountain in front of Sweet Valley Middle School. She couldn't wait to tell her fellow Unicorns about the rock concert, not to mention her new plans for the future. They were going to be so jealous.

"There's Amy," Elizabeth said, catching sight of her best friend, Amy Sutton. "We have to go see Mr. Bowman to talk about this Friday's cover story. See you later, Jessica."

"OK," Jessica answered distractedly. She quickly scanned the crowd of students clustered around the fountain. When she spotted Lila Fowler, her best friend, she waved and ran directly to her.

"Hi, Lila." Lila had been checking her shoulder-length brown hair in a small mirror. She put the mirror into her handbag and looked up at Jessica.

"Hi. Why are you dressed like that? Going to a costume party?"

Jessica frowned. "Of course not," she said. "I'm dressed just like the greatest rock singer alive. Can't you tell?"

She twirled around so Lila could see the full beauty of her outfit. The scarves fluttered around her neck, and the layers of necklaces tinkled softly.

"If you'd been to the concert last night, you'd understand," Jessica added.

Lila pouted. "It's not fair! You won free tickets. That concert sold out two minutes after tickets went on sale. I can't believe I, of all people, couldn't get a seat." Her father was one of the wealthiest men in Sweet Valley, and Lila was used to getting anything she wanted.

"The concert was incredible," Jessica said. "Even better than a Johnny Buck concert. *We* had front-row seats."

"I know. You've told me four times already," Lila grumbled. "I suppose Melody sang all the songs from *Powerful*?" *Powerful* was the name of Melody's newest album.

"Oh, yes. She sang every single one. And they sound much better in person," Jessica told her. "Not that the record isn't great, too, of course. But there's something about a live performance—"

"Sure, sure," Lila said. "Listen, about our Unicorn meeting—"

Ellen Riteman and Mary Wallace, two more Unicorns, appeared at the other end of the school yard and came quickly to join them.

"Jessica, you look great. Just like Melody Power," Mary exclaimed. "Wasn't the concert tremendous?"

"You were there, too?" Lila raised her dark brows.

"Yes. I went with my stepfather," Mary said. "He's a bigger fan than I am. We both thought Melody was incredible."

"I had front-row seats," Jessica reminded them. "And Melody looked right at me."

"You're so lucky." Mary sighed. "We sat pretty far back. I could hardly see Melody's face."

"I saw everything," Jessica boasted. "Look, see how I've knotted my scarves? This is exactly how Melody wears hers."

"Wow!" Everyone except Lila crowded around to examine Jessica's handiwork. Just then they all heard the shrill sound of the school bell.

"I'll tell you more about the concert at lunch," Jessica promised as she started toward the school entrance.

Lila shrugged. "But we have an important Unicorn meeting at lunchtime. I wanted to talk about our next party—"

But for once the other girls weren't interested in what Lila had to say.

"That would be fantastic, Jessica," Ellen agreed. "You can show us how to tie that knot."

"Definitely," Jessica said. She wasn't going to say anything, but she didn't think this new style of dressing would suit just anyone—only rock stars in training. Still, it wouldn't hurt to share *some* of her new tips with her friends. "And you haven't heard the best part yet."

"What?" Ellen demanded. "You didn't get to *meet* Melody Power after the concert, did you?"

"Well, no," Jessica confessed. "But this is even better. I've decided that I'm going to be a rock star, too."

"Wow!" Mary's eyes widened.

"Are you serious?" Ellen asked. "That's not easy to do."

"Forget it, Jess. You'll never make it," Lila said.

"I will, too," Jessica assured her. "I'm already making plans."

"I can't wait to hear about it. See you later,

Jess," Mary said, heading for her seventh-grade homeroom.

Ellen, Jessica, and Lila hurried toward their own classroom. Lila didn't seem to be in any rush to hear about her plans, Jessica noticed. She was probably just jealous. Even though Jessica had only a vague idea of how a person became a rock singer, she was sure she'd think of a good plan very soon.

That night at dinner, Jessica displayed her new style to the rest of the family. "Isn't it great?" she asked her father, twirling to show off her whole look before she took her seat at the table.

Mr. Wakefield had a twinkle in his eyes. "Definitely far-out," he told his daughter.

"D-aa-d, you're so old-fashioned," Jessica said, searching his face to see if he was teasing her.

Steven let out a huge guffaw and said, "Jessica, what happened to you? It looks like your whole closet fell on your head."

"This is the Melody Power look, you dummy," Jessica said indignantly.

"Yeah, well, a rock star can get away with wearing that kind of stuff," Steven said. "But you look like an alien creature!"

"I do not! All the Unicorns think I look great,"
Jessica informed him. "What do boys know about
fashion, anyway?"

"I know enough not to wear thirteen different
colors at one time," Steven argued.

"OK. That's enough," Mrs. Wakefield warned.
"I'd like to eat dinner in peace, please."

Steven turned his attention to the chicken and
mashed potatoes on his plate. But Jessica wasn't
ready to admit defeat. "Besides, *I* am going to be a
rock star," she said. "So I can dress any way I
want!"

Steven laughed so hard that he started to cough.
"You—a rock star! What a joke."

"Just wait. You'll all be sorry you didn't take
me seriously!" Jessica shouted.

This time it was her father who frowned at
her. "Jessica, it's not necessary to raise your voice.
And Steven, don't laugh at your sister."

"I can't help it. She's so funny," Steven announced. "She can't even sing."

"I can too sing. I had the lead in the fifth-
grade musical," Jessica reminded him. "And I had
that role in *Carnival*. I'm in the choir, too, Steven.
You don't know anything."

"She's right," Elizabeth observed. "She has a
nice voice, Steven, and you know it."

"Maybe. But the school play isn't exactly the big time." Steven bit into his second piece of chicken. "I don't think the recording companies are standing in line waiting to sign Jessica to a contract."

"Well, everyone has to start somewhere," Jessica pointed out. "At least I know what I want to do."

"Sure, just like a few weeks ago, when you decided you were going to be a great actress." Steven grinned at his sister's angry face.

Jessica looked toward Elizabeth for support, but her twin seemed torn.

"That was just a passing idea," Jessica said, defending herself. "This time I'm sure!"

"Then we wish you luck," Mr. Wakefield told her, smiling. "I'll be the first in line to buy tickets to your concert."

"Thank you, Daddy." Jessica felt better. What did Steven know, anyway?

"But if you don't eat your dinner," Mrs. Wakefield added, "you'll never have the strength to make it to the recording studio."

Jessica took a bite of her chicken, ignoring her brother as he smirked on the other side of the table. She'd show him!

By Friday, even Jessica's friends were starting

to lose interest in her new plans. At lunch, Jessica and her friends sat at their regular table reserved for the Unicorns in what they recently had named the Unicorner. When she offered to show Ellen how to do her hair just like Melody Power's, Ellen shook her head.

"I don't think so," she told Jessica, putting her sandwich wrapper back into her lunch bag. "If I sprayed my hair purple, my mom would kill me."

"Well, we could leave off the color," Jessica suggested. "My mother wasn't too excited about that part either. Look, all you have to do is use a lot of gel and brush your bangs back—"

"Really, Jessica," Lila interrupted, setting down her carton of fruit juice, "give us a break. We're getting tired of hearing about nothing but Melody Power."

Jessica bristled. "Just because *you* didn't get to go to the concert—" she began, her tone huffy.

"I wish you hadn't gone either," Lila retorted. "Then maybe you could talk about something else once in a while."

Jessica jumped up and put her hands on her hips. "Some friend you are. You're just jealous because *I'm* going to be the next Melody Power."

"Dressing like a rock star doesn't turn you into one, you know!" Lila exclaimed.

Jessica glared at her friend. Didn't anyone take her plans seriously?

A voice from behind them interrupted their argument.

"Here's the new edition of *Sweet Valley Sixers*," Mary Wallace called.

All three girls turned eagerly to take a paper from the pile Mary had brought over.

Jessica glanced at the front page, eager to read Elizabeth's article on the concert. To her surprise, the headline on the front-page article read, "SVMS Student Leads Food Drive for Homeless."

The rock concert story was on page two. Jessica shook her head. *Leave it to Elizabeth to mess up*, she thought. Jessica left the rest of the Unicorns browsing through the paper and went to find her sister.

"How do you like the paper, Jess?" Elizabeth asked, looking up as Jessica stalked into the newspaper office.

"Great, huh?" Amy Sutton added, pushing her blond hair out of her face. "We did a good job this time, don't you think?"

"It would have been a lot better if the concert story had appeared on page one," Jessica told them. "How could you put such an important story on an inside page?"

Elizabeth tried to explain. "Come on, Jessica. Randy Mason's idea for the food drive was really important. The sixth grade collected three boxes of canned food for the food bank."

"That isn't as exciting as a rock concert!"

Amy shook her head. "Exciting isn't everything, Jessica."

"Amy's right, Jess. And this story was the first in a series of Star Student articles," she told her sister. "It was my idea to interview students with outstanding accomplishments and run the stories on the front page."

Jessica suddenly forgot about her complaint. "Really? Maybe you'd like to do a story about me next? After all, I'm an up-and-coming rock star," Jessica argued. "That's worthwhile."

"When you're successful, then we'll write a story about you," Amy stated bluntly.

Jessica felt her face flush, and her anger returned full force. "If you don't believe me—" she began.

Elizabeth grabbed her sister's sleeve. "Come on," she told her. "Lunch period's almost over. We'd better get to class."

Jessica followed the other two girls into the hallway, but she soon lagged behind them. Elizabeth and Amy were already sitting at their desks by the time Jessica reached the classroom. As she entered, the slight breeze from the door fluttered a paper pinned to the bulletin board. Jessica glanced up at it.

"Girl singer wanted for new rock band," the paper said. "Auditions Saturday."

Jessica's eyes widened. This was it—her big chance!

Three

◇

Jessica was so excited she could hardly believe what she had read. But it was still there: "Girl singer wanted for new rock band. Auditions Saturday." She read the rest of the handwritten announcement quickly.

"Ahem." Someone coughed gently. "Miss Wakefield, do you plan on joining us today?"

Looking up, Jessica saw Mr. Nydick standing in the doorway, waiting to shut the classroom door.

"Sorry," she said, flashing her teacher a brilliant smile. She hurried to her desk and sat down. Mr. Nydick returned to the front of the room and began his class. Jessica found it impossible to pay attention to the history lesson. Who cared about ancient Rome when her big moment had arrived? This was it, a chance to become a rock singer, the first step on the road to stardom.

Jessica smiled happily, lost in her own dream world. She'd show everybody!

"Well, Jessica?"

"What?" She sat up straighter, suddenly aware that Mr. Nydick had called on her.

"I said," he repeated, "what did they call the emperor of the Roman Empire?"

Jessica, still caught in her daydream, blurted out, "Rock star?"

The rest of the class let out a great shout of laughter. "All hail the great rock star!" Jerry McAllister said under his breath. He made bowing motions. The other students laughed even harder.

"That will do."

Mr. Nydick glanced around the room. Although the noise quickly died down, the teacher looked stern. "I do not approve of ill-timed jokes," he told Jessica. "I'll see you after class, Miss Wakefield."

Jessica refused to worry. Mr. Nydick's bark was always worse than his bite. She quickly returned to her dreams. How many sports cars would she own when she became famous? And how many houses filled with closets of fancy clothes?

When the final bell rang, Jessica reported back to Mr. Nydick. Her punishment was that she would have to stay after school for one hour, reading her history assignment.

When Jessica's detention was over, she hurried home. She opened the kitchen door and smelled the aroma of freshly baked cookies, but her mother didn't seem to be home. Mrs. Wakefield worked part-time as an interior designer at Sweet Valley Design. She probably had an appointment with a client.

Jessica grabbed a cookie and ran upstairs to her pink-and-white bedroom. She had plans to make, practicing to do. As she munched on the cookie, she pushed a pile of clothing off her bed. Searching through a stack of magazines, she finally located her new Melody Power album, *Powerful*. She slipped it onto the turntable and turned on the stereo.

Waves of music filled the room. Standing in front of the mirror, she struck a suitable pose, one hand on her hip, and began to sing loudly along with the tape.

"What are you doing?"

Jessica glanced over her shoulder. Elizabeth stood in the doorway, frowning.

"I live for love!" Jessica belted out. She stopped singing long enough to answer. "What does it look like I'm doing?"

"It sounds like you're making a terrible racket," Elizabeth said.

Jessica's mouth dropped open. "Are you jealous, too?"

"What?" Elizabeth shook her head. "I can't hear you." She walked across the room and turned down the volume.

In the sudden silence, Jessica's voice came out louder than she meant it to. "Why did you do that?"

"So we can talk. First you get in trouble at school—" Elizabeth began.

"Oh, that was nothing." Jessica shrugged off the incident. "Mr. Nydick wasn't really angry."

"He did a good imitation, then. You were supposed to answer 'Caesar,' you know."

"Who cares about people who've been dead hundreds of years?" Jessica asked. "I have more important things on my mind. Listen, can you keep a secret?"

"What are you up to, Jessica Wakefield?" Elizabeth asked. "You're not planning something outrageous, are you?"

"Elizabeth, just listen," Jessica interrupted. "This is something really great—my big opportunity. It won't be a secret for long. Soon all of Sweet Valley will know, and Mom and Dad will be proud of me."

Elizabeth relaxed. She sat down on the edge of her twin's rumpled bed. "OK, tell me."

"Four boys at school are starting a rock band," Jessica said. "Isn't it wonderful? And they're the cutest boys in school, too! Bruce Patman, of all people!"

"I think he's really stuck up," Elizabeth said. "I thought you didn't like him much either, after he teased you at his last party."

"Well, he's still the cutest boy at school," Jessica said. "People do make mistakes, you know. Even I've made some."

Elizabeth let out a giggle, but Jessica hurried on. "He's got the most beautiful blue eyes—"

"Who else is in the band?" Elizabeth asked. "Because if you're depending on Bruce Patman to get a band started, you may wait a long time."

"Oh, there's Aaron Dallas, Peter Jeffries, and Scott Joslin."

Elizabeth looked impressed. "Scott's pretty good. And Aaron's taken piano lessons for years. They're really starting a rock band?"

Jessica nodded emphatically. "And they're auditioning for a singer. Tomorrow! I've got a lot of practicing to do before tomorrow afternoon."

"Is that what you were doing?"

Jessica frowned. "Come on, Lizzie. You said yourself I have a nice voice."

"Yes, but what I heard didn't sound like singing. It was more like growling," Elizabeth objected.

"That's how Melody Power does it," Jessica said. "She has that incredible low, gravelly voice. Don't you remember?"

"But why do you want to sound like her? Don't you think you should sound like yourself?"

"Of course not, Lizzie. Not if I want to be a rock star." Jessica looked at herself in the mirror, practicing her stance.

Elizabeth made a face at her sister's reflection. "But when you sang in the school show—"

"You heard what Steven said—that was kid stuff. This is totally different."

"I don't think so."

"Believe me, I know more about it than you do," Jessica assured her twin. "This is how it's done. And I can't wait to join the band. They're calling it *NRG*."

"What?"

"Say it fast and run it together; it sounds like *energy*, get it? What do you think my professional name should be? Jessica's too ordinary."

Elizabeth looked worried.

Jessica felt a flicker of alarm. "What's wrong now?" she demanded.

"I heard some of the girls talking about the audition after school today. I didn't pay any attention, but now I know what they were talking about. There will be some pretty good singers there, Jessica."

"Like who?"

"Well, Dana Larson, for one. She got the lead

in the school musical that you wanted, remember? And Sandra Ferris—she's had private voice lessons."

"Oh, I'm not worried." Jessica felt her moment of doubt fade. She glanced back at the mirror. "After all, Lizzie, it takes more than a good voice to be a rock star."

"It does?"

"Sure. It takes a special kind of person with— you know—*charisma*." Jessica twirled; she loved to hear the tinkling of her jewelry, to feel the soft flutter of the layers of scarves. "I mean, look at me. Some of the girls at school are copying me already. Can't you just tell that I'm meant for stardom?"

Elizabeth had to laugh. Her twin certainly had plenty of confidence. "I hope you're right, Jess."

"Sure I am," Jessica predicted. "Now go away, so I can rehearse!"

Four

◇

By Saturday afternoon Jessica's throat ached from the strain of imitating Melody Power's singing style. But if her voice sounded a little husky, so much the better. It was more like Melody's voice that way. She was bound to get the position with the band. What could possibly go wrong?

Jessica dressed even more carefully than usual for the audition. She spent extra time fussing with her layers of scarves and necklaces, and added a couple of charm bracelets that jangled nicely when she waved her arms. Today, her entire outfit was even more outrageous.

When she arrived at Bruce Patman's house, she was panting from riding her bike so fast. The luxurious Tudor-style home was even larger than Lila Fowler's house. The Patmans were probably the wealthiest family in Sweet Valley, and Jessica couldn't help feeling impressed by the big house and broad sweep of the carefully groomed lawn.

She walked her bike up the long drive and continued around to the side of the house. The side door was open, and a hand-printed sign said, "Auditions in the basement."

Jessica hurried down the steps. She found three other girls already there. She knew Dana Larson and Sandra Ferris. The other girl was a seventh grader whose name she didn't remember.

"Hi. Have the auditions started yet?" Jessica asked Dana in a low voice.

Dana shook her head. "The boys are still setting up their equipment," she told Jessica. "But they should be ready soon."

Jessica sat down beside Dana. She noticed Dana's blue jeans and simple cotton sweater. *And Elizabeth thought she would be serious competition?* she thought to herself.

Across the room, the boys appeared very involved with their tasks. Bruce Patman was tightening a string on a bass guitar, frowning as he adjusted it to his liking.

Jessica sighed happily. Bruce was the best-looking boy in the seventh grade, maybe even in the whole school. He had the clearest, most incredible blue eyes. The pale-blue sweater he was wearing set them off perfectly.

Aaron Dallas was a muscular sixth grader who kept his brown hair cut short. He was bent over his electric keyboard, muttering to himself. Peter Jeffries, also a sixth grader, fingered a guitar. And Scott Joslin, a seventh grader, was setting up an impressive set of drums. He checked the cords leading to the large amplifiers, then struck the bass drum hard. Sound boomed through the basement.

"Wow," Jessica murmured. "This is going to be great."

Unfortunately, not everyone in the Patman family appeared to share Jessica's appreciation for rock music. She heard a door shut quickly, then the tap of high-heeled shoes on the basement stairs.

"Bruce," someone called, "I want to see you, please. Right now."

"Oh, no," Bruce muttered. "It's my mom."

He slipped the guitar strap from around his neck and laid the guitar on the nearest chair. He went up the staircase and disappeared from sight. Jessica strained to hear the conversation.

"I told you," Mrs. Patman was saying, "my committee is meeting again this afternoon."

"But, Mom, we have to rehearse. And the auditions—" Bruce argued.

"I'm sorry, darling. But you know what Mrs. Wallington and Mrs. Seager said last time your band played during our meeting. They couldn't hear a thing we discussed."

"But, Mom—"

"You know I wouldn't discourage you normally," Mrs. Patman said, sounding torn. "But this is my first year to head the Charity Ball Committee, and Mrs. Wallington has been on the board for twelve years."

"Just because your friends can't hear very well—" Bruce began, his tone resentful.

"Now, Bruce. Your band will just have to wait until the Charity Ball is over."

"But that's three months away!"

"I'm sorry, dear. There's nothing I can do. Oh, there's the doorbell. I must get upstairs. Please tell your friends, Bruce."

Jessica had overheard the entire conversation. This was terrible! What about her plans?

Bruce came back into the basement, his shoulders sagging. "Bad news, guys," he told the other band members. "My mom says we can't rehearse here. What about your house, Aaron?"

"You kidding? My mom would never let us in the door. She hates rock music. Thinks I should stick to Bach, classical stuff like that."

Bruce made a face. "Yuck. What about you, Peter?"

Peter shrugged. "My house doesn't even have a basement. And the family room's not big enough."

Scott looked worried. "We can't rehearse at my house, either. My next-door neighbor has a new baby, and Dad said we can't make a lot of noise."

"Looks like our band isn't going very far," Bruce told them, his voice gloomy. "Who ever heard of a silent rock band?"

Jessica couldn't stand it any longer. "What about the auditions?" she called, jumping up and hurrying over to the boys. "Don't I get to sing?"

Bruce frowned at her. "Didn't you hear what I just said? We won't have any place to play."

"You could have the auditions at my house." Jessica smiled, pleased with her brilliant idea. "We have a huge basement with plenty of room."

"Are you sure?" Bruce stared at her. "What about your parents?"

"Oh, they won't mind," Jessica promised, her tone airy. "My parents are pretty cool. And they like all kinds of music."

Bruce began to look more hopeful.

Jessica thought rapidly. "In fact, if I were a member of the band, you could practice at our house any time you wanted. Every day, even."

Bruce looked around at the other boys. "What do you say, guys? Want to try Jessica's house?"

Scott nodded. "Sure. Why not?"

The boys began to disassemble their instruments.

"I'll go ask our gardener to give us a ride over in his van," Bruce said. "Who wants to carry all this stuff?"

Curled up on her cream-colored bedspread, Elizabeth turned a page of her book. She loved mysteries, especially ones by Amanda Howard. This one was a real thriller. She was totally absorbed in the story when a large boom shook the house.

Elizabeth shrieked and dropped her book. "Oh, no!" she gasped. Were they having an earthquake?

But thankfully the bed remained still and firm beneath her. She looked around the room; nothing was shaking.

"But—" Elizabeth began, puzzled, when another loud noise made her jump to her feet. *Bam!* Was it an explosion? It sounded as if it had come from the basement. Elizabeth hurried down the staircase and opened the door to the basement. The noise was deafening. She took a deep breath, then descended cautiously, pausing on the landing to peer into the basement.

"Jess, is that you?"

Jessica, who had been dancing madly to the music, stopped long enough to wave at her sister. "Hi, Lizzie."

"I might have known." Elizabeth walked down

the rest of the steps. "What's going on? Oh, hi, Dana. Hi, Sandra."

Elizabeth nodded to the rest of the girls sitting in the room. She couldn't really greet them because the music was so loud. Jessica walked over and yelled into her twin's ear. "I'm just getting into the mood."

"For what?"

Jessica giggled. "Guess what? The band needed a place to hold the auditions, so I told them they could use our basement."

"Did you ask Mom?"

"Oh, she won't mind. Didn't Steven and his team lift weights here while the weight room at school was being painted? No one complained about that."

"But lifting weights isn't this noisy," Elizabeth pointed out. She shuddered slightly as Bruce Patman hit the wrong note on his bass guitar. "Why didn't they rehearse at one of the band members' houses?"

"It's a long story." Jessica waved her arm, making her bracelets shake. "I'll tell you later. Right now I have to get into the mood for my song. I'm going to try out in just a minute. Want to wait and watch me?"

"I guess so," Elizabeth agreed. She sat down on the steps. Jessica danced to the music, mouthing the words to the song under her breath. The other girls were humming along with the music.

Elizabeth bit her lip. It was easy to see how much getting this position with the band meant to her sister. She just hoped that Jessica wouldn't be disappointed.

A few minutes later, Bruce announced, "OK. We're ready to play."

Elizabeth had her own opinion about that, but she kept her mouth shut. She was anxious about Jessica's chances. How would Jessica handle her disappointment if she wasn't the one chosen to sing with the band?

"Who wants to go first?" Bruce asked. "We're going to play 'You're the One,' like we agreed earlier."

"I'll go first," Dana said. She walked across the room to take the small, hand-held mike. "Ready?"

Bruce nodded and struck a chord on his guitar. The other boys joined in and Dana began to sing.

Elizabeth felt her heart sink. Dana was good. Her voice was clear and strong, and she really seemed to know what she was doing. Elizabeth glanced at her sister. Could Jessica top this?

Jessica was last to sing, so Elizabeth had to sit patiently through the next two auditions. Both were pretty good, but not as impressive as Dana.

"Your turn, Jessica," Bruce said at last.

Elizabeth held her breath. When Jessica began to sing, Elizabeth cringed. She wanted to jump up and run across the basement floor, grab her twin, and give her a big shake.

Jessica usually had a nice, sweet voice. The hoarse, artificial voice she was using now, in imitation of Melody Power, didn't sound like Jessica at all. It didn't sound like Melody, either. It just sounded awful.

But Jessica seemed quite pleased with her performance. She gave one last flourish and took an exaggerated bow as she ended her song.

"Thanks, girls. We'll just go out to the backyard and discuss the tryouts in private before we announce our final decision," Bruce explained. "Come on, guys."

The rest of the band laid down their instruments, and they all trooped out of the basement.

Elizabeth waited for her sister to sit down beside her. "Don't feel bad if you don't get it, Jess," she whispered to her twin. "You tried hard. And *I* thought you sounded good."

That wasn't exactly true, but Elizabeth thought she might as well say something nice, since Jessica was bound to be disappointed when she wasn't chosen to be the band's singer.

"Thanks. I did, too," Jessica said matter-of-factly. "I can't wait for them to announce their decision."

Elizabeth nodded. What could she say?

Just then, to her surprise, Bruce and Aaron and the other two boys came back down the steps.

"Wow. That was fast," Elizabeth murmured in surprise.

"We've made our choice," Bruce announced, looking important.

All the girls tensed.

"I just know I've got it," Jessica whispered to her twin. She squeezed Elizabeth's arm in excitement and bounced up and down a little.

Elizabeth braced herself for the worst.

Five

◇

"Thanks for coming," Bruce said at last. "You were all good. But we've decided that Jessica should be the singer for our band."

"I knew it!" Jessica shouted. She threw her arms around her sister and gave her a big hug.

The other girls congratulated Jessica and headed for the stairs.

Elizabeth was too surprised to say anything for a moment. When she finally got over her shock she said, "Good going, Jess. Congratulations."

Elizabeth noticed that the other three girls didn't seem to be taking the news too hard. She saw the girls out, then hurried back down the stairs.

Jessica was talking to Bruce, gazing adoringly into his eyes. Bruce nodded, then turned back to the rest of the band.

"We'll have a rehearsal tomorrow afternoon," he announced. "Everybody be here by three."

"I'm so excited, Elizabeth," Jessica said, coming up beside her twin. "Now I'm really on my way to becoming a rock star, just like Melody Power! Isn't it great when your dreams start to come true?"

Elizabeth nodded and smiled at her sister, but all of a sudden she started to get a funny feeling in her stomach. Did Jessica's selection have anything to do with the band's rehearsing in the Wakefield basement? She felt even more suspicious when Scott called, "Hey, Jessica, is it OK if I leave my drum set here? I don't want to have to drag them around. My parents won't let me practice at home anyhow."

"Oh, sure," Jessica assured him. "Our parents won't care. Will they, Lizzie?"

"I suppose not," Elizabeth agreed.

When the four boys climbed the stairs, Jessica followed, talking to them animatedly. She was busy making plans for the band's future, but the boys didn't linger to hear her ideas.

When the door shut behind them, Elizabeth couldn't remain silent any longer.

"Jess! Did you tell the band they could practice in our basement?"

"Sure. What's wrong with that?" Jessica picked up the last cookie and took a big bite.

Elizabeth regarded her sister sternly.

"Oh, sorry. Did you want half?" Jessica flashed a charming smile and broke off part of the cookie, offering it to her twin.

Elizabeth shook her head. "No, thanks. But I want to know: Did you tell them they could rehearse in our basement before or after they selected you to be their singer?"

"What difference does it make?" Jessica shrugged. "I got the job, didn't I?"

"It makes a lot of difference, Jess," Elizabeth argued. "Bruce may have picked you for the wrong reason."

"Don't be silly. I would have been chosen to be their singer either way." Jessica sounded certain. "Talk to you later, Lizzie. I've got a lot to do."

"Going to practice your singing some more?" Elizabeth asked hopefully. Maybe now that Jessica was past the audition, she would drop that terrible voice imitation. If only she would go back to her own more natural singing style, she'd sound much better.

"No way. I don't have time for practicing right now. I have to go through my closet and decide what to wear to rehearsal tomorrow. If I'm going to be a rock star, I have to look the part, you know." Jessica skipped out of the kitchen.

Elizabeth sighed. If Jessica was determined to

believe that Bruce had chosen her for her voice rather than for the use of her basement, there was nothing Elizabeth could do to change her mind.

She headed upstairs to her bedroom, suddenly remembering the mystery novel she had abandoned when she heard the commotion from the band. She'd better hurry up and finish it. It looked as if quiet time would be scarce around the Wakefield household for the next few weeks.

On Sunday afternoon, NRG assembled in the Wakefield basement as scheduled. Once again the house shook with their loud but unpracticed tunes.

Upstairs, Mr. Wakefield emerged from his study, shaking his head. "Are you sure we knew what we were doing when we okayed this?" he asked his wife.

Mrs. Wakefield sat in the family room. Elizabeth was curled up on the sofa beside her. They had been trying to watch a nature film on TV, but found it impossible to hear the narrator.

Mrs. Wakefield smiled. "It's good for them," she promised. "Besides, wouldn't you like to discover you'd nurtured the next teen idol?"

"Heaven forbid," Mr. Wakefield said, rolling his eyes. "I think I'll just run down to my office for a while."

"What time will you be home, dear?"

"Well, what time is the rehearsal going to end?"

"Five-thirty."

"Fine. That's exactly when I plan to be home." Mr. Wakefield winked at Elizabeth, then collected his briefcase from his study.

Mrs. Wakefield laughed. "I think watching television is a lost cause," she told Elizabeth. "Maybe the music won't sound quite so over-whelming if we go outside."

Elizabeth wasn't as sure. "Guess I'll go see how they're doing," she decided.

When she opened the basement door, the music was deafening.

"Wow!" Elizabeth exclaimed out loud. "Sounds like they're trying to make up for lack of talent with volume."

All four boys seemed very absorbed in their tune. Elizabeth had expected to find her sister in the midst of the band, practicing her lyrics.

Instead Jessica knelt at one corner of the basement.

Elizabeth approached her. "What are you doing?" she yelled.

"Painting the band's name on the guitar cases," Jessica shouted back. "See? Doesn't it look nice?"

Elizabeth nodded. Jessica had lettered the name NRG very neatly on the two black cases. But why hadn't the boys done it themselves?

"Why aren't you singing with the band?" she asked.

"Oh, the guys needed to work on their chords first," Jessica explained. "I'll start my song in just a minute. I'm almost done here."

But by the time Jessica finished her lettering, Bruce had thought of another chore for her to do. When the band took a break, he called across the room.

"Would you ride to my house for me, Jessica, and ask my mom to look in my bedroom for my extra pick? I was in a hurry to get here and I forgot it," he explained.

Elizabeth raised her eyebrows. Did Jessica have to run all the band's errands, too? What about her singing?

But Jessica seemed happy to help. "Oh, sure," she agreed quickly.

"Good. And hurry, will you?"

"I'll be as fast as I can," Jessica promised. She pushed back the paints and brushes, then scrambled to her feet and headed for the stairs.

Elizabeth followed. "Really, Jess," she whispered. "Shouldn't Bruce be doing this himself?"

"Oh, I don't mind," Jessica said. "It just proves how much he trusts me, don't you see?"

Elizabeth wasn't sure that she did. "I guess it's all right to run his errands if it doesn't bother you," she said. But as she watched her sister climb on her bike and head for the street, Elizabeth grew even more suspicious of Bruce and his band.

On Monday afternoon, the band gathered after school to rehearse once more in the Wakefield basement. But just as Jessica stepped up, ready to sing, Bruce stopped her.

"Hey, Jessica, I just broke a string. Could you go to the music store and buy a string to replace it? I'll give you the money."

"OK," Jessica agreed. "But we'll have to practice my songs when I get back."

"No problem," Bruce said.

But by the time Jessica made the trip, selected the guitar string, then rode home, the band was ready to stop for the day. Puffing from her energetic pedaling, Jessica looked disappointed.

"What about my songs?" she demanded. "I haven't rehearsed yet."

Bruce said, "Sorry, Jessica. Scott has to be home by six-fifteen. But we'll play your songs first when we practice tomorrow afternoon, I promise. You've been a real help to us, you know."

Jessica brightened at once, forgetting her moment of resentment. "I'm just doing my part," she assured him. "After all, we're a team. I mean, a band." She giggled.

"Right," Bruce agreed quickly.

"Do you have any more of those great cookies we had yesterday, Jess?" Scott asked.

"I think so. Let me check the kitchen. I'll see what I can find," Jessica told them.

In a few minutes she came back down the steps with a plateful of cookies.

"Wow, this is terrific," Peter told her.

"Yeah, Jess," Bruce said, chuckling. "You're a real *gem*, as my grandmother would say."

The other boys snickered at Bruce's teasing, but Jessica didn't even seem to notice. She grinned broadly. "Hey, maybe I could use that as my stage name. *Gem!* What do you guys think?"

Bruce started to laugh, then turned the sound into a cough. "Uh, sure, Jessica. Whatever you say."

Six

◇

Although Jessica didn't spend much time practicing, she spent plenty of time talking about her big plans. Even Elizabeth began to get bored with her twin's constant chatter about becoming a rock star.

"NRG's going to go far," Jessica told her family at dinner.

"I wish they'd go farther to rehearse," Steven grumbled. "Like, to the next town. I can't even hear my stereo when they play."

"Why do you need to turn on your stereo when you've got a great band in your own house? I thought you liked rock music." Jessica frowned at her brother.

"I do. I just don't call what your band makes *music*," he told her.

"For your information, the band's songs have incredible harmonies!"

"Say that again?" Steven paused, his fork halfway to his mouth.

Apparently pleased at his surprise, Jessica smiled. "Their overtones may be a little bit harsh, but they're working on them," she informed her family.

Mr. Wakefield looked amused. "Since when did you develop such technical expertise?" he asked his daughter.

Elizabeth turned to stare at her sister. "It's those music magazines you've been reading, isn't it?" she guessed. "I saw them on your bed."

Jessica nodded. "I have to understand my chosen field, don't I?" she said reasonably. "And have I told you what my stage name is going to be?"

"Stage name?" Mrs. Wakefield looked alarmed. "What's wrong with the name you've got?"

"Jessica's all right for everyday. But it's much too ordinary for a rock singer," Jessica explained. "What do you think of the name Gem?"

Steven leaned back in his chair and laughed heartily.

Jessica pouted, throwing her brother an indignant look.

"Well, I'm glad that the band is making so much progress, dear," Mrs. Wakefield said. "You must be working very hard."

"Oh, I am," Jessica said. She picked up her fork and began to eat her dinner.

Seated beside her sister, Elizabeth didn't say a word. Their parents hadn't been down in the basement to see what was really going on.

What will happen if the band ever has a chance to actually perform? Elizabeth wondered. *Doesn't Jessica realize how awful she sounds?*

After school on Tuesday, Amy went home with Elizabeth. They filled a plate with Mrs. Wakefield's freshly baked oatmeal cookies, poured two glasses of milk, and climbed the stairs to Elizabeth's room. Elizabeth handed Amy her latest Star Student interview and flipped through her notes while Amy read it.

"You did a good job interviewing Peter DeHaven," Amy said, handing the pages back to Elizabeth. "This is going to be an interesting article."

"Thanks. The pen pal club was a lot of fun to talk about. I told Peter about your pen pal. He said you could join the club even though you've been writing to her for a few months. How is Samantha, anyway? I haven't heard you talk about her lately."

Amy frowned. "That's because I haven't heard from her in a while."

"I'm sure you'll get a letter soon. Well, I'm ready for a refill. Want some more milk?"

Amy nodded. They headed for the kitchen, where they took a few more chewy oatmeal cookies from the cookie jar.

Then Jessica burst into the kitchen, emptied the entire cookie jar onto a plate and took an assortment of soft drinks from the refrigerator.

"The band needs some refreshment," she explained, turning back toward the basement. "I'm just about to do my first number, you guys. Why don't you come listen?"

"OK. We'll be right there," Elizabeth agreed, although she didn't really want to see her twin ordered around by Bruce again.

After Jessica disappeared with her armload, Amy whispered, "How are things going with the rock band? I've heard Jessica talking at school about how much the band depends on her."

"Yes, she does seem to think that." Elizabeth let out a sigh. "Oh, Amy. I don't understand why Jessica doesn't see how badly Bruce and the other boys are treating her. They make her run all their errands and wait on them hand and foot. And her singing—"

Elizabeth hesitated. She didn't like to criticize her own sister. "Well," she said, "maybe it's getting better. Let's go see."

But when the two girls slipped quietly down the basement stairs, Elizabeth's dismay returned. Jessica had just approached the microphone. She held it close to her mouth and swayed as she sang.

If you could call it singing, Elizabeth thought to herself.

Jessica seemed to growl and sputter, trying to deepen her voice to match Melody Power's singing style. And the way she drew out all her vowels—

"I li-i-i-ve for lo-o-o-ve," Jessica ended, practically howling when she got to the final notes.

Elizabeth had to struggle not to hold her hands over her ears.

Bruce Patman shuddered, but Jessica was facing her audience, and didn't see him.

Jessica grinned and bowed. Then she turned to the band. "How'd I do?" she asked.

Peter and Aaron refused to meet her eye. Scott leaned over his bass drum, seeming intent on some minor adjustment to his foot pedal.

"You sound just like a real pro," Bruce Patman assured her.

Watching from the end of the basement, Elizabeth saw Aaron's face turn pink at this incredible statement.

"Thanks," Jessica said to Bruce. "Can we do my next song now?"

"Uh, not right now, Jess," Bruce said. "You sound fine, but we need a lot more practice on our instruments."

"Oh. All right," Jessica said, looking disappointed. "Maybe tomorrow we'll have time to go over more of my songs."

"Sure," Bruce agreed. He turned back to the other boys with obvious relief.

Elizabeth looked at Amy and shook her head. What could Jessica possibly be thinking?

"Hi. Like our show?" Jessica asked, coming over to where Elizabeth and Amy were standing.

For once, even Amy seemed at a loss for words. "Umm, it's different," she managed to say.

Jessica turned to her twin. "What do you think, Lizzie? Don't I sound just like Melody Power?"

"Well, not exactly," Elizabeth hedged. "Don't you think you should sound like yourself?"

Jessica looked indignant. "We've been through this before. You just don't understand what it takes to be a rock singer, Elizabeth."

"I suppose not," she said, giving up hope. "But I still think they should let you practice with them a little more."

"Well, it doesn't matter. I've got other things to do."

Jessica pointed to a few jars of paint and a pile of blank colored paper. "See? I'm making posters to advertise the band," she explained. "Publicity is really important for a rock band." Jessica sat down on the floor and began to paint.

Elizabeth and Amy hurried back up the stairs. When they reached Elizabeth's bedroom, Elizabeth sank onto her bed, finally allowing her distress to show.

"I don't know what to do!" she told her friend. "Should I tell Jessica how awful she sounds?"

"I don't think it matters," Amy pointed out. "You know she's not going to listen to you."

Elizabeth groaned. Poor Jessica. For her twin's sake, Elizabeth had to hope the band never got a job. She was sure Jessica would never survive the humiliation.

Jessica spent the next hour working on the posters. By the time the band left, she had a stack of them completed. She climbed up to the kitchen to call to her sister.

"Elizabeth, come look!"

When Elizabeth reached the basement, Jessica asked, "Don't they look good?"

Elizabeth inspected the posters. "They do. Good job, Jess."

"NRG—the newest sound in rock!" the poster read. "Sweet Valley's own rock band." In equally big letters, the next line announced, "With its star singer, GEM."

Elizabeth grinned. Trust Jessica not to leave herself out.

In smaller print at the bottom, Jessica had painted, "Available for parties and other events. Call for information." The Wakefields' phone number was written at the bottom.

"Now what?"

"I'll make more posters tonight," Jessica vowed. "Then I have to get these out where they can be seen. Tomorrow, after our practice session, I'll hang them all around town. You can help, if you like."

The following afternoon, Bruce was so taken with the posters that he urged Jessica not to waste any time getting them downtown.

"We can rehearse your songs any time," he told her. "Better hang these right away."

Jessica felt pleased that her posters were such a big hit. "I'll start right now," she said.

"Terrific. Uh, Jessica, how about bringing us some sodas before you leave?"

"Sure." Jessica hurried up the steps and rummaged through the refrigerator. She took an armload of soft drinks down to the basement.

Then she picked up her stack of posters and headed for her sister's room.

"Are you coming with me, Lizzie?" Elizabeth sat at her desk, hard at work at her electric typewriter.

"Sorry, Jess. I need to finish this story for the school paper."

"Another star student? Who is it this time?" Jessica paused long enough to peer over her twin's shoulder at the sheet of paper in the typewriter.

"Peter DeHaven started a pen pal club. Students from Sweet Valley Middle School are making friends all across the country. I've been thinking of looking for a pen pal who lives in Alaska. Don't you think it would be exciting to find out what it's like there?"

Jessica shook her head. Elizabeth had the strangest taste. "I can't see what is so exciting about a letter-writing club. I still think you should write an article about our rock band," she grumbled. "Especially when your own sister is the star singer."

Elizabeth looked down at the floor. "Well, Jess," she said, "it's not as though the band is actually performing. So far, all they've done is rehearse in our basement. And eat all our cookies," she added.

Jessica tossed her blond hair. "You'll see,"

she promised. "I'm taking the bus to the mall to pass out my posters. We'll have our first gig before you know it."

"Gig?"

"That's music talk for job," Jessica said.

"Oh. Right." Elizabeth tried to smile as she turned back to her typewriter.

Jessica went back downstairs. She rolled up her stack of posters carefully and placed them in her lavender backpack. Then she headed for the bus stop.

Many of the store owners knew her, so she didn't have much trouble persuading them to accept her posters once she arrived.

She stopped at Casey's Place first, an old-fashioned ice cream parlor that was one of the favorite gathering places for Sweet Valley Middle School students.

"A local band? Sure, Jessica. I'll put it in the window," the manager agreed.

"Thanks a bunch," Jessica said, smiling brightly. She said goodbye and headed for the next shop. The next three stores all took posters. After she visited several more stores, Jessica's knapsack was empty. Exhausted, she ran for the bus stop when she saw the bus approaching.

"Where have you been, Jessica?" Mrs. Wakefield asked as Jessica entered the kitchen. "Dinner's almost ready. I was getting worried."

"Didn't Elizabeth tell you? I had to go to the mall." Jessica explained that she had been putting up posters for the band.

Mrs. Wakefield smiled. "You certainly have worked hard at promoting your band, Jessica. I'm really proud to see you devoting so much time and energy to your project."

Jessica smiled happily. If her mother was proud of her now, she thought, just wait till the band's first performance. Someone was sure to call after seeing her posters. Soon Jessica would be singing before a real audience!

Seven

◇

When the phone rang on Friday night, Jessica hurried to answer it. "Hello?" she said. "Yes, this is the right number."

The conversation lasted only a few minutes, but Jessica was grinning broadly when she hung up.

"NRG has their first gig," Jessica announced to her family triumphantly. "All thanks to my publicity!"

"Wow, Jess, I'm impressed," Steven admitted. "I didn't think you'd actually get a real job."

"I guess the band picked the right person when they chose you to be the singer," Elizabeth said.

Jessica nodded. "Of course they did. Now I've got to call Bruce."

She hurried back to the phone and dialed

Bruce Patman's number. When she broke the news, there was a long silence at the other end of the line.

"Bruce, did you hear me? I said we have a job. The band has a gig. We're going to play at a birthday party."

"A real job? They're going to pay us?"

"Of course. It's not very much, but it will be great publicity. And I bet we get more jobs after this, better paying ones, too."

"Wow, I can't wait to tell the guys."

"I can call them if you like," Jessica offered.

"No. I'll do it. See you tomorrow afternoon at rehearsal."

"Right."

Jessica hung up the phone, feeling left out once again. Bruce hadn't said a word about how important her posters had been in obtaining their first job. He hadn't even thanked her for all her hard work.

The next afternoon when the boys gathered in the basement, again Jessica's contribution seemed to be overlooked. None of the band members seemed to realize that they would never have gotten the job if it weren't for her posters.

"I knew we'd get to perform," Aaron was saying.

"Yeah," Bruce said. "When you're hot, you're hot, right? News was bound to get around."

"It got around a lot faster because of my posters," Jessica couldn't help saying.

"Huh? Oh, yeah. We have to really work hard, guys. Only a week until the party."

"Do you think we'll be ready?" Scott asked, worried.

"We have to be," Bruce told them. "Otherwise, we're going to look pretty silly."

This thought made all the boys turn very serious.

"Get to work on your fingering, Peter," Bruce commanded.

"You're a great one to talk. You're the one who can't get the intro right," Peter retorted.

"Come on, guys," Scott begged. "We've got to work together. We can't waste time arguing."

"Right." Bruce nodded. "Let's take it from the top."

"How about me, Bruce? When can I sing?" Jessica demanded.

"You know we need more practice than you do," Bruce replied. "We have to decide the order of the songs we're going to play, too."

"And when I get to do my solo," Aaron reminded him.

"Yeah, and what about the number with my drum solo?" Scott put in.

Jessica sighed and sat down. These rehearsals were starting to get a little boring. Then she had an idea.

"Well, if you're going to work on that stuff first," she interrupted, "I'll go over to Lila's house for the Unicorn meeting. I've missed two already, and the girls are getting mad—"

"What? And miss rehearsal?" Bruce looked outraged.

"But you just said—"

"I don't care. We might need you around. What if I break a string, or something?" Bruce argued. "You have to be here, just in case, Jessica."

You could take care of it yourself, Jessica thought, frowning.

"Besides, who cares about a dumb club?" Bruce added. "You've got more important things to do."

"Right. Think we could have something to drink, Jessica?" Scott asked. "I'm so thirsty, I can't concentrate."

Jessica trudged up the steps toward the kitchen. "Honestly," she griped aloud. "The Unicorn Club is not dumb. It's important. And Lila's hardly speaking to me because I've missed so many meetings."

"Why are you talking to yourself?" Elizabeth asked, coming into the kitchen.

"Oh, I'm not," Jessica said quickly. She wasn't about to start complaining to her sister that being a rock singer wasn't as much fun as she thought it would be. "I'm just getting the guys something to drink."

She took an armload of soft drinks down to the basement. Instead of thanking her, Bruce complained. "Don't you have any more root beer, Jessica? I hate ginger ale."

"Sorry, we're out," Jessica told him. *Mainly because you've been drinking it all,* she thought. But she bit back her quick answer and sat down to wait for her chance to sing.

On Tuesday Bruce arrived with a portable cassette player. "Look," he told the others, "I had a great idea. I'm going to tape our session. Then we can hear how we sound, see what we need to work on the most."

"Good thinking, Bruce," Aaron said.

The other members of the band agreed. Jessica could hardly wait to hear herself singing. For once, Bruce didn't waste any time. The band played through their whole list of tunes, finally allowing Jessica to sing her two biggest numbers at the end of the tape.

She gave it all she had, real Melody Power style. She had hoped to do a few more songs, but the tape ran out. When she put down the portable mike attached to Bruce's recorder, Bruce hurried to rewind the tape.

The rest of the band put down their instruments and gathered close to listen. When the tape began to play, Bruce frowned at the mistakes he had made with his guitar lead-in. The sour notes made them all wince.

"Guess I'd better do some work on my fingering there."

Jessica nodded. It was amazing how much more obvious the mistakes sounded on tape. She was glad she wasn't playing an instrument. Singing was different.

They listened to three more songs. Then Scott glanced at his wristwatch.

"It's almost six," he exclaimed. "I've got to get home."

The other boys stood up, too. "It doesn't matter. We've almost finished the tape," Bruce said.

"But we haven't listened to *my* songs," Jessica protested.

Bruce shrugged. "We'll hear the rest tomorrow." The rest of the band headed for the stairs and Bruce turned to follow.

"Wait, Bruce," Jessica said. "Let me keep the tape. I can listen to the rest of it on my own tape player."

"All right, Jess. See you tomorrow. And everybody be on time. We only have a few more days to rehearse."

As soon as the boys were out of the house, Jessica hurried upstairs to her bedroom. She slipped the tape into her tape deck and fast-forwarded until she found her song. She stood in front of her full-length mirror so she could practice dancing to her singing. Then she waited, eager to hear how she sounded.

She almost fell over when she heard the voice that came out of the speakers. Screeching, shrill, wobbling into the lower ranges and back again, it didn't sound anything like Melody Power's voice. And it didn't sound like Jessica's, either. She had to put her hands over her ears to drown out the horrible sound. When she could stand it no longer, she jumped up and turned off the tape player. Pacing up and down, Jessica bit her lip to keep from crying.

How could she have been so stupid? She had thought she would sound so glamorous. Instead, she sounded completely foolish.

She would never live it down. She had told all

her friends about her singing, about what a star she was going to be. What would they say when they heard her?

Jessica drew a deep breath, trying to think calmly. It was Tuesday already. The birthday party was Saturday afternoon. She had only four days to practice, and the other band members were so concerned with their own rehearsing, they would never allow her enough time to sing.

She would just have to do it on her own, Jessica decided. Shutting her bedroom door firmly, she rewound the tape. She would work on singing the lyrics to the other songs on the tape. She would start over, from scratch. Jessica pushed the button and began to sing, softly at first.

Not too bad, she thought. At least she sounded more like the old Jessica. But her voice was too weak. Nobody would be able to hear her.

She turned the tape over so she could record herself, then took a deep breath and started again. She remembered what her choir teacher had said at school about *projecting*: "Breathe deeply and aim at the end of the room." Jessica tried to project her voice, but it wobbled uncontrollably.

This was hard!

She tried again, then listened to the recording. This time she sounded better, but could use a little more expression. She had to find her own style. She remembered what Elizabeth had tried to tell her about using her own voice. If only she had listened to her then. Jessica hoped it wasn't too late.

Eight

◇

After school on Thursday, Lila Fowler was standing beside Jessica's locker when Jessica got there. "I suppose you're gong to skip our Unicorn meeting again," Lila said angrily.

"I have to, Lila. The band is rehearsing this afternoon," Jessica explained.

"That's all you do lately," Lila complained. "You must be the best singer in California after all this practice."

Jessica didn't say anything. Once she would have agreed with Lila, even though she knew her friend meant to be sarcastic. But now—should she tell Lila the truth? No, it was too humiliating.

"I can't help it. Honest. You know I would come if I could. But our first job is Saturday afternoon at Simon Holliday's birthday party."

"That name sounds familiar." Lila pursed her lips. "Do I know him?"

"I don't think so. He goes to private school," Jessica added quickly. "And he's only going to be eleven. That's why his mother decided to give our band a chance. She thought we'd be perfect, since we're almost the same age."

Lila didn't seem to be listening. "I'm sure I've heard of him. Oh, I know," she said, snapping her fingers. "His family belongs to the same country club as me and my dad. I bet I could get an invitation to his party."

Jessica stared at her friend, not at all pleased with this suggestion. She didn't want anyone she knew to hear her sing. "Why would you want to do that? It's only a fifth grader's party."

"But it's your singing debut. I want to hear you. Giving up so many club meetings must be worth something! I mean, if you're really going to sing."

"Of course I'm going to sing!" Jessica retorted.

"Well, I'll see what I can do about getting invited. Hey, if you can't come to our meeting this afternoon, what about coming over to my house tonight? We could practice putting on makeup."

"Not on a school night," Jessica said quickly. "I have too much homework to do."

That wasn't exactly true, but Lila seemed to accept it. "Yeah, I guess you haven't had much time for your homework either. Honestly, Jessica, you're turning into a real bore. All you do is practice, practice, practice. I guess I'll have to ask Ellen to come over instead.''

"Whatever you want." Jessica tried to shrug off Lila's comments, but her friend's remarks stung.

When all of the Unicorns headed for their meeting, Jessica walked home alone. She hated missing the time with her friends, but what else could she do? She had to practice!

Later that night, after the band's rehearsal and after dinner was over, Jessica locked herself in her room again for another session of private practice. But she'd hardly begun when someone knocked on the door.

"Jess, can I come in? It's me, Elizabeth."

Jessica opened the door.

"Mom's taking me to the mall. Do you want to come?"

Jessica wavered. Shopping was her all-time favorite thing to do, after Unicorn meetings. But Saturday was only two days away. She sighed and shook her head.

"I can't. I have work to do."

Elizabeth looked surprised. "If you say so. I'll tell Mom. See you later, Jess."

*   *   *

At the mall, Elizabeth could hardly concentrate on her shopping. She couldn't imagine what had come over Jessica. It wasn't like her to pass up a shopping trip. Elizabeth sighed. She looked through a rack of sweaters, but nothing seemed right.

"Have you decided, Elizabeth?" her mother asked. "That blue one is nice; it brings out the color of your eyes."

Elizabeth shook her head. "It's pretty, but I can't make up my mind."

Mrs. Wakefield glanced at her watch. "I have to walk down to the Outdoor Shop and pick out some new jeans for Steven. He seems to outgrow his every other week. Why don't you look around some more and make up your mind? I'll meet you in front of Valley Fashions in twenty minutes, OK?"

Elizabeth nodded.

As her mother walked away, Elizabeth looked through the rack of clothing one more time. She still wasn't satisfied. She had seen a pretty sweater at the shop next door. She decided to go look at it again before making her final choice. As she walked toward the front door, she heard a familiar voice.

"What about this one, Bruce? Think it looks right for a rock band?"

"Naw," Bruce Patman scoffed. "That's old-fashioned. Keep looking."

"How about Hawaiian shirts?" Aaron Dallas suggested. "With black jeans."

"I don't think so," Peter Jeffries argued. "I like these blue and red shirts."

"Solid black would be cool," Scott Joslin said. "We have to look different."

"Yeah, we could paint our faces," Bruce agreed, his tone sarcastic. "Wear purple wigs."

All the boys laughed at his wit.

Elizabeth was intrigued. This was Jessica's band—Bruce Patman and the other three boys. Why were they out shopping for band costumes without Jessica?

Luckily, the boys hadn't noticed her because of a rack of clothes standing between them. Elizabeth didn't like eavesdropping, but she felt something was wrong about the whole situation.

"I can't wait till Saturday afternoon," Aaron said. "We're going to be terrific."

"Yeah," Scott agreed. "Everybody in Sweet Valley will hear about NRG. They'll all be talking about our band, and how good we are."

"We'll probably have someone from Los Angeles coming out to sign us to a recording contract," Peter added. "Maybe we'll be on TV."

Bruce nodded his agreement. "We're pretty hot, all right. Good thing I had the idea to start the band."

"Hey," Scott objected, "I had the idea first."

"Yeah, but I had a basement to practice in," Bruce pointed out. "Well, I thought I did."

"Good thing we found Jessica," Peter observed. "She sure can't sing, but at least she gave us a place to practice."

Elizabeth made a face. She knew it! Bruce and the others had been using her sister, just as she'd suspected all along. Wait till she told Jessica!

She started to move away, but the next comment made her freeze.

"How are we going to keep Jessica from singing at the party on Saturday?" Aaron sounded worried.

"Yeah," Peter said. "She'll spoil our whole show."

"Don't worry," Bruce assured them. "I'm way ahead of you. I've got the whole thing figured out."

"Tell us," Scott demanded. "I've been worrying about that, too. We can't let Jessica ruin our performance."

Ruin it! Elizabeth fumed. *How dare they?* Then she remembered how terrible Jessica's new style of singing sounded. She could hardly blame them. Still, she felt herself tense when Bruce went on.

"I'm going to tell Jessica to come at three-thirty," he told the other boys. "She's never on time, anyhow."

"But I thought we were supposed to be there at two," Scott said.

"That's the whole idea, dummy." Bruce chuckled. "Don't you get it? By the time Jessica arrives, we'll almost be done with our performance. Then nobody will have to listen to her sing."

"She's going to be mad," Aaron warned.

You don't know the half of it, Elizabeth agreed silently. *What a dirty trick to play on Jessica!*

Bruce laughed. "So what? We'll tell her she got the time wrong. She can't prove we did it on purpose. And after this show, our band will be so famous, we won't need Jessica anymore. We'll be able to rent rehearsal space."

"Great idea, Bruce." Peter's tone was admiring.

"Hey, I'm not your fearless leader for nothing," Bruce boasted. "Now, which shirts are we going to get? We have to look special."

Elizabeth fumed while the boys finally agreed on blue shirts trimmed in red. While they picked out the right sizes, Elizabeth slipped away, thankful that none of the boys had caught a glimpse of her.

She couldn't believe the boys thought they could get away with treating her sister so badly. Elizabeth stormed out of the store, then took a deep breath. *Those rats!* she thought.

In the next shop, she found a red sweater with a blue design that would complement the boys' band costumes perfectly. When Elizabeth met her mother back at Valley Fashions, Mrs. Wakefield agreed that Elizabeth had made a good choice.

On the way home, Elizabeth began to worry. She had planned to storm straight up to Jessica's room and tell her the whole story. But now she had second thoughts.

If Bruce carried out his plan, Jessica would definitely be heartbroken. But if Elizabeth told her twin the truth and explained how the band had been using her, Jessica would be even more devastated. Jessica thought she was a valuable member of the band, and she'd been very proud of her participation.

And then there was her singing. Bruce had said some terrible things. He had even admitted using Jessica just so the band could practice in the Wakefields' basement. But Elizabeth had to admit he was right about one thing: Jessica's singing. Her sister sounded terrible! The audience would think so, too. They might even laugh at her. Or boo her!

Elizabeth made up her mind. She wouldn't say a word. The boys' scheme would go ahead as they planned. Jessica would miss the performance, but maybe that was the kindest thing to do.

Elizabeth hoped she was making the right decision.

Nine

◇

On Friday afternoon, Elizabeth and Amy walked out of school together after the last bell rang.

"Isn't it great? A whole weekend with no homework!" Amy exclaimed. "Why don't you come over to my house, Elizabeth? We could play a game of Monopoly before dinner. You still owe me about two million dollars from our last game."

Elizabeth giggled. "You're right," she agreed. "Guess I should try to get out of debt."

The two girls had started to walk down the steps when Elizabeth saw Jessica and Lila come out of the big double doors.

"Just a second, Amy. Let me tell Jessica where I'm going." Elizabeth ran back up the steps.

"Hey, Jess!" she called.

"Hi, Elizabeth."

"I'm going over to Amy's for a while. Tell Mom where I am, would you?"

Jessica nodded. "Sure, Lizzie."

"Are you going to a Unicorn meeting?" Elizabeth asked, looking from one girl to the other.

Lila tossed her brown hair, her expression disdainful. "Are you kidding? Miss Rock Star here is too busy for Unicorn meetings lately. She even turned down an invitation to a sleepover tonight at my house with all the other Unicorns."

"I've got too much to do," Jessica murmured. "Maybe next time."

Elizabeth saw how unhappy her sister looked. It took a lot for her to pass up a sleepover with the Unicorns. Elizabeth felt a renewed pang of sympathy when she thought about how badly Jessica wanted to become a rock star. Now she wasn't even going to make it to the band's opening act.

"Got to go. The band will be waiting for me," Jessica said, running off.

Lila sniffed. "If she's half as important to that band as she thinks she is, they must not be able to play a single note without her." Lila walked away, too.

Elizabeth watched her sister go. Had she made a mistake by not telling her twin what she had overheard at the mall the night before?

Amy came to join her. "Is something wrong, Elizabeth?"

"Yes. I can't decide whether or not I'm doing the right thing about Jessica."

"What do you mean?" Amy asked.

Elizabeth considered confiding in her friend, but after a moment, she decided she'd better not. "Uh, I have to think about it some more before I tell anyone."

"Oh, well, I hope you make the right choice."

"Not half as much as I do." Elizabeth sighed. "Come on, let's get to that game. I need something else to think about."

When they reached the Sutton home, Amy stopped long enough to look through the mail on the kitchen counter.

"Darn," she murmured.

"What's wrong?"

"I still haven't gotten a letter from Samantha. She used to be so good about writing. I wonder if anything's wrong."

"Oh, Amy, you sound like me. Don't be such a worrywart," Elizabeth teased her. "You'll probably get a letter from her tomorrow."

When Elizabeth got home later that afternoon, she was relieved to see Bruce Patman and the other boys in the band just leaving. She didn't even want to say hello to them after the way they had treated her sister.

Where was Jessica, anyhow? Elizabeth glanced into the kitchen. She could tell that the boys had made their usual raid on the plate of cookies Mrs. Wakefield always left for her children. The kitchen was empty.

Elizabeth climbed the stairs slowly, trying to think of what she would say to Jessica. She had to wish her luck for the performance tomorrow, act like she expected her twin to do well. She couldn't reveal that she knew that Jessica wouldn't even get to sing!

But Jessica wasn't in her bedroom. Where was she?

Elizabeth went back to the staircase. Steven was probably still practicing basketball, her mother had an appointment with a client, and her dad was still at work. The Wakefield home was very quiet. But a faint murmur of sound rose from the basement.

What was that? The band had left; Elizabeth had seen them go. She tiptoed down the stairs until she reached the basement door. She eased it open, and peeked inside.

At the other end of the big room, Jessica stood in front of a portable tape recorder, singing softly along with the tape.

Elizabeth's eyes widened in surprise. Jessica sounded good! She had finally dropped the phony Melody Power imitation. Her singing sounded more like her old voice, but even better.

Had Jessica been practicing in secret all this time?

Elizabeth shut the door and tiptoed back up the stairs. Now she felt even more confused than ever. If Jessica could give a good performance tomorrow, it was truly heartless to allow the boys to trick her out of her big chance in the spotlight.

But if Elizabeth admitted that the boys had been using Jessica all along, her twin would be so upset, she still might not be able to sing.

What on earth should Elizabeth do? How could she possibly avert disaster for her sister?

Ten

◇

"Lizzie?" Jessica called from the patio.

Elizabeth shifted slightly on the low branch of the big pine tree in the backyard. This was her thinking seat, a spot she visited when she had things to straighten out or difficult problems to solve. She'd been sitting there for twenty minutes already and she still hadn't made any decision about what to tell Jessica about the band performance.

"Eliza—oh, there you are." Jessica stuck her head in between two branches and smiled at her twin. "Dinner's ready."

"I'm coming," Elizabeth said.

She slid off the branch and followed her sister inside. But when she sat down at the dinner table, she found she had no appetite. She picked at her meal and continued to think about her problem.

As soon as dinner was over, Jessica disappeared again. This time Elizabeth knew where her sister had gone. Elizabeth went up to her room and tried to read her Amanda Howard book. But it was no use. She just couldn't concentrate. When she finally gave up and got ready for bed, she heard the creaking of her twin's bed as Jessica tossed and turned on the other side of the bathroom door.

Elizabeth couldn't bear it any longer. She tiptoed into her twin's room.

"Jessica? Are you awake?" she whispered.

In the dim light of the moon she saw Jessica sit up in bed.

"Oh, Lizzie. I'm so nervous about the show! I'll never get to sleep, and I'll be too tired to sing well tomorrow. I'm going to sound terrible!" Jessica wailed.

"Shh, Jess. Don't worry about it. You'll do fine." Elizabeth hesitated. "Listen, I have something to tell you."

She saw Jessica grow tense. Her expression became even more alarmed. "What is it? Tell me."

Elizabeth took a deep breath.

"What?" Jessica repeated.

"I heard you practicing this afternoon, by accident. You sounded really good."

Jessica's anxious expression dissolved into a dazzling smile. "You mean it?"

"Cross my heart. Your singing is better than ever."

Jessica relaxed and sank back onto her bed. "Oh, Lizzie. I feel so much better now. Thanks."

Elizabeth smiled at her sister. "Now get some sleep."

She turned back to her own bedroom and crawled into bed. Now Jessica could rest easy, but Elizabeth still had her terrible secret hanging over her.

The next morning, Jessica was up early. After an early-morning practice session in the basement, she ate a piece of toast and then began to prepare for her big performance.

Elizabeth watched her sister closely. It was now or never. What should she do?

Jessica scrubbed her face, then twirled a strand of blond hair around an electric curler. When her whole head was a mass of curlers, she poked her head through the bathroom door. Looking like Frankenstein's bride, she yelled to her sister, "Did anyone call for me, Lizzie? I thought I heard the phone ring while I was in the basement."

"No, that was for Dad," Elizabeth told her.

Then she sat up very straight, riveted by a sudden idea. At last, she knew what to do!

"Oh, you did have a phone call." Elizabeth jumped off the bed. "Bruce left a message; you're to be at the party at two o'clock instead of three-thirty."

Jessica's mouth fell open. "And you almost forgot to tell me! How could you? You could have made me miss the whole performance!"

Elizabeth didn't flinch under her sister's angry gaze. "Well, you know now," she pointed out. "And the band is wearing blue shirts with red trim."

"What? Why didn't he tell me that yesterday?" Jessica looked down at her T-shirt and mini-skirt. "I won't match at all. What am I going to wear?"

"Don't worry," Elizabeth assured her sister. "I've got the perfect outfit."

She rummaged through her bureau until she found the new red-and-blue cotton sweater. Pulling it out, she brought it to show her sister. "You can wear my new sweater. It'll be perfect for the show."

"Well," Jessica said thoughtfully, glancing down at her outfit. "But what about all my scarves and necklaces?"

Elizabeth raised her eyebrows, but she didn't say a word.

"Oh, I know." Jessica sounded cross. "You're going to tell me that I should stop imitating someone else. Even if Melody Power is a rock star, it doesn't mean that I should try to look like her."

Elizabeth grinned. "It's up to you."

"I guess the sweater would look good on me," Jessica agreed. "And with a silver necklace, and that Indian belt Dad bought me in Arizona—"

She began to change clothes quickly. After some anxious rummaging through both their closets, and with Elizabeth's help, she was ready by one-thirty.

When she was finished, she went back to the mirror to inspect her outfit.

"You look terrific," Elizabeth told her sister, her tone completely sincere.

Jessica regarded her reflection in the mirror. She had on the red sweater with the blue design, her blue denim miniskirt, blue suede shoes, a silver and coral belt, and a silver necklace with matching bracelets borrowed from Elizabeth. "I do look good, don't I?" she said.

"You'd better go," Elizabeth warned. "You don't want to be late for your first gig, do you?"

Jessica giggled.

"What's so funny?"

"You, trying to sound like a rock music expert."

Elizabeth smiled at her twin. "We can't all be rock stars, I guess."

"Oh, Lizzie." Jessica suddenly clutched her sister's hand. "I'm nervous again. My stomach is doing flip-flops. What if I forget all the words to my songs? What if they don't like my singing?"

"They'll love you," Elizabeth said firmly. "Now go."

"Why don't you come with me?" Jessica looked alarmed at the thought of going alone.

"I wasn't invited," Elizabeth pointed out. "And I'm not part of the band."

"Sure you are," Jessica argued. "We'll say you're my personal assistant." She smiled at her sister and they both laughed.

"OK," Elizabeth said. "I'm dying to see the show. Let's go!"

They rode their bikes to the site of the party. It was a large house not far from Bruce Patman's. As they rode into the driveway, they heard music coming from the backyard. They parked their bikes and walked around to the back of the house, where they saw a swimming pool and a spacious deck.

Walking closer, they saw a big tent sheltering tables of soft drinks, sandwiches, and a big birthday cake. Balloons decorated the edges of the tent and hung from the trees and the fence. A few even floated in the pool. A large group of kids had gathered around the refreshment table. Some of them were making faces at the band. Elizabeth didn't blame them. The band sounded pretty bad.

"I don't know why Mom and Dad didn't get a *real* band for my party," said a blond-haired boy who was standing near the twins.

Jessica was quick to defend her band. "They're just getting warmed up," she told the birthday boy. "Give us a chance, will you?"

"Who are you?" he demanded.

"I'm Gem, the band's vocalist," Jessica told him, sounding important. "I promise you're going to enjoy the show."

Elizabeth stood a little to the side, but she could clearly see the surprise on Bruce's face when Jessica threw her head back and walked straight through the crowd of kids up to the band. Several of the guests stared at her curiously.

Elizabeth grinned. Trust Jessica to make a grand entrance.

The boys in the band gaped at her, too, but Jessica, busy arranging her microphone, didn't seem to notice.

"So there, Bruce Patman," Elizabeth murmured

under her breath. She stepped back and found a place to sit.

"Oh, hi, Elizabeth. What are you doing here?" someone said beside her.

Elizabeth turned and saw Lila Fowler sitting on a deck chair, sipping a glass of punch. "Lila? I didn't know you were coming to the party. I came to hear Jessica sing, of course."

"Well, unless she's better than the band, the show may not last very long," Lila predicted. "Everyone's grumbling about the music."

Elizabeth crossed her fingers and said firmly, "I'm sure Jessica will change everyone's mind."

Lila shrugged. "We'll see."

The band finished its number with a couple of ragged notes. Bruce must have noticed that the audience was not exactly impressed with the band's playing so far, because he no longer wore that confident look. He nodded at Jessica who then joined the band members to confer.

"This is, uh, Gem, our singer," Bruce announced weakly a few minutes later. He waved to the band, and they began the next number. Jessica took a deep breath and began to sing.

The first notes were soft, but then her voice swelled. Elizabeth could hear the words perfectly from where she sat at the side of the yard. Her twin's voice was clear and sweet.

Around Elizabeth, the kids murmured to each other. Elizabeth was almost afraid to look at them. What if they didn't like Jessica?

Several kids began to move to the beat of the song, and two girls at the front of the crowd began to dance.

Elizabeth grinned. They liked Jessica's singing!

The frowns and bored expressions had disappeared. More and more of the kids began to dance. Simon, the birthday boy, looked pleased at last.

When Jessica sang the last words of her song, a strong wave of applause swept through the crowd. "Yeah, Gem!" someone called.

Elizabeth looked around. What an ovation! The crowd of kids looked really pleased. She swallowed hard, releasing her last bit of anxiety, and clapped along with the rest. "Way to go, Jess!" she yelled across the yard.

Even Lila was impressed. "Boy, I didn't know Jessica could sing that well," she said. "Wait till I tell the other Unicorns!"

But Elizabeth hadn't waited to hear what Lila was saying. She hurried toward the band, eager to congratulate her sister.

Jessica grinned as she approached. "How'd I do?"

"You were terrific; even better than in rehearsal," Elizabeth told her honestly.

"I think it was the stage fright," Jessica whispered, giggling. "I had to try even harder to overcome it."

"More!" someone in the crowd yelled.

Bruce looked positively stunned. "Wow, Jessica," he said. "I didn't know you could sing like that. I mean, you've really improved. I just wish we'd rehearsed with you some more."

Jessica answered in a cool voice. "Don't worry. I've been working on my own. I can sing along with any of the tunes you've been practicing." She turned to the band. "Let's do the second song now, the one with the drum solo." She nodded graciously to Scott, who gripped his drumsticks nervously.

Scott looked guilty. "We did that one already, just before you came," he confessed. "And I was so nervous, I messed up my solo."

"Don't worry," Jessica assured him. "Now that I'm singing, it'll go much smoother. This time, I'm sure you'll do fine."

Elizabeth glanced at Bruce. She was taking great pleasure in his discomfort. He didn't seem to know whether to be angry or relieved.

Another look at the restless crowd seemed to help him make up his mind.

"Let's hear Gem again," someone called. "She's good!"

"Ready?" Bruce asked Jessica, watching her anxiously for a cue.

"Ready!" Jessica said.

As soon as she started to sing again, the guests went wild. Everyone joined in the dancing and Elizabeth sat back and watched her sister bask in the spotlight.

Eleven

◇

All day long on Monday everyone at Sweet Valley Middle School was talking about NRG's performance at the birthday party.

"Jessica was really good," Elizabeth told Amy and Mary Wallace at lunch. "And if she hadn't been, I think the band would have been in big trouble, because they were awful!"

Amy laughed. "After all the bragging Bruce Patman did, to think that Jessica saved him."

Mary nodded. "But he doesn't seem to have learned much. I heard him boasting about the band's great future while I waited in the lunch line."

"You're kidding." Elizabeth shook her head. "I thought he'd learned something from their performance Saturday."

"Well, he learned one thing. He's now talking about NRG and *Gem*," Mary told them.

All the girls laughed at the thought of Jessica's stage name.

"I bet Jessica feels pretty proud," Amy said.

"Are you kidding?" Elizabeth lifted her milk carton and drank the last of her milk. "I promised to do an article about the band in *Sweet Valley Sixers*. And yesterday Steven told her that if her head got any bigger, she'd lift the roof right off our house."

Mary and Amy laughed. At the sound of the bell, they picked up their trays and hurried toward the disposal conveyer.

In the halls that afternoon, Elizabeth heard more gossip about the band—and Jessica's great show.

"I heard my brother say the band might be asked to play for a high school party," Betsy Gordon said between classes. "But only if Jessica sings, too. She was the best one in the band, I heard."

"That's true," Elizabeth agreed solemnly. "I was there."

She was glad to see Jessica getting full credit for her effort at last. But Jessica had said very little about the rest of the band yesterday. Elizabeth was curious to see what her twin would say to Bruce.

After school, Elizabeth invited Amy over so they could see how things went at rehearsal, now that Jessica was the star.

When they reached the Wakefield home, Elizabeth found the boys already in the basement, ready to go to work.

"Is Jessica here?" she wondered aloud, as she and Amy came down the steps. "I hope she's not waiting on the band hand and foot again."

Amy whispered, "I don't think so." She pointed to the other side of the basement.

Elizabeth's eyes widened. Jessica was sitting in the middle of the band. Scott was trying a sequence on his drum.

"What do you think about that, Jessica?" he asked eagerly. "Should we try that in our next song?"

"Maybe," Jessica considered.

"What about this lead-in?" Peter demanded. "Listen to this, Jessica, and tell me what you think."

"No, let her listen to my new piece first," Aaron argued.

Elizabeth and Amy glanced at each other. "Where's Bruce?" Elizabeth wondered.

They found out almost immediately. Elizabeth heard someone else coming down the stairs, panting a little.

"I got your lemonade, Jessica, and some cookies," Bruce said as he hurried across the basement.

"Those aren't the right kind," Jessica said, shaking her head. "I told you to look in the right side of the pantry."

Bruce frowned. "Oh, sorry. I'll go look again." He hurried back up the stairs.

"Boy," Amy said quietly to Elizabeth. "Looks like Jessica's a star, all right."

"You can say that again," Elizabeth agreed. "Serves them right!"

They watched the band rehearse several songs, while all the boys listened anxiously to Jessica's advice.

"Guess what, guys," Bruce said. "Johnny Gordon called me about the band—and Gem"— he glanced quickly at Jessica— "performing for a high school party. How about that?"

"Wow. We're really moving up," Aaron said.

The other two boys nodded, but Jessica shook her head. "Sorry," she told Bruce. "I can't make it."

"But they don't want us without—I mean," Bruce stuttered, "you don't even know when the party is going to be."

Jessica shrugged. "It doesn't matter. I'm not singing with the band any more."

"What?" Bruce looked shaken. The other three boys appeared just as surprised.

"It was fun and all, but being a rock star is just not what it's cracked up to be. I've never worked so hard in my life! And besides, I've missed all the Unicorn meetings and two parties. You guys can continue without me, of course." Jessica tried to look modest, but didn't quite succeed.

"But—" Bruce seemed stuck. "We can still rehearse in your basement, can't we?"

Jessica shook her head. "Sorry," she told them. "The Unicorns are on the way over right now. I told them we'd work on our next party at my house, and we need the room. Guess you'll just have to find a new singer with a big basement."

"Why didn't you tell us before we lugged all our equipment back over?" Aaron asked.

"Well, I wanted you all to be here for my announcement. And I thought you could use my advice today after what happened on Saturday."

The band members groaned.

"Here come the Unicorns now," Jessica said when she heard footsteps on the basement stairs.

"Hi, Jessica," Lila Fowler greeted her as she came closer. "I'm sorry we missed your rehearsal."

Ellen Riteman and two other Unicorns added their quick agreement.

"That's OK," Jessica said. "I'm tired of singing. Look, I've got this great idea for our party." She glanced over her shoulder. "The boys are just leaving."

Their expressions sour, the boys began to dismantle their equipment.

"I guess Gem and NRG are history," Elizabeth said as she and Amy retreated quietly up the stairs. "Serves them right for the way they treated her."

Amy nodded.

"Do you want something to eat, Amy?" Elizabeth reached into a cabinet for a package of crackers and set them on the counter beside a pile of mail. When she saw it, she remembered Amy's concern about her pen pal. "Hey, did you get a letter from your pen pal yet?"

Amy looked glum. "No," she said. "I didn't. she hasn't answered my last three letters. I wonder what's happening. I'm going to write to her again. If she doesn't answer this time, I don't know what I'll do."

"I'm sure she's OK," Elizabeth assured her.

But she noticed that Amy didn't look so certain.

Where has Amy's pen pal gone? Find out in Sweet Valley Twins #35, AMY'S PEN PAL.